I0714008

Alone on the Yellow Stone

Cover art by Douglas C. Granum.

Cover design by Scott Norris

douglasgranum.com | monkeyhouse-media.com

ISBN 978-1-939723-12-3

First Edition

DOUGLAS C. GRANUM

Alone on the Yellow Stone

Somewhere, someone is undressing. Somewhere, the sun is setting for someone.

While somewhere, someone is traveling alone.

Somewhere, someone thinks of a drawer long unopened, where things lie that haven't seen the luminous light of day for many years.

In this drawer, at the bottom of an old inherited French bureau, are treasures with the promise of release.

There are things in this drawer that ravens like. Things that are shinny, oiled, black, like the raven. There are chambers filled with eternity, colored papers with writings that speak of love and loathing.

In this disordered drawer are small, brightly colored ribbons, now faded, bits of broken beach glass of purples and greens, a ball of string, delicate, pretty ruined feathers, little abstract bits of shinny jagged metal, sort of a bowerbird's nest, along with rigid, desiccated food, chewing gum, old and brittle, stuck to its wrappers, and finally, little hairy dustball men.

Ultimately, digging to the very bottom, a lethal blued steely .357 Smith and Wesson pistol, along with a box filled with .357 copper jacket hollow points.

As I sit in my driveway in my old plum crazy purple 70 Hemi Cuda, its engine running roughly, struggling, gasping for oxygen, at idle in the icy air, its 426 dual four barrel carbs thirsty, sucking fuel, I think about her, sleeping there in the house. I think about me.

I hate this moment, thinking for all my hopes of love and warmth there will be isolation, that I will be alone.

She, whom I fell in love with for all the right reasons, will also be alone. That all of our dreams, gentle, tender, loving moments, hopes for the future, shared memories of the past, all of this, what is all of this? This, crumbling, cracking, twisting, and finally falling, what fell?

I, alone as a man is without a woman. Alone as a face in a rain-beaded window, where I have been crying so much since you have been gone. I can't cry any more, can I?

Small glistening salty pools fill my eyes, run down the slopes of my cheeks, and once more, I choke, weep, gasping out, "Oh, goddamnit," sobbing.

I have never spent one day in this life

that I haven't rejoiced for its beauty, feared for its fragility, and prayed for the future. What am I doing? What have I done?

She there, quietly sleeping, is alone, as only a woman can be alone in her bed, lying on her side, knees pulled up. Alone like the rest of mankind, always in some need of healing.

Man is a little world adrift on the infinite.

When your heart is an icy mist of freezing static, thoughts have no edge. You are endlessly exposed. You are frightened that your one and only precious life will always be this way.

Crying in your presence, I simply won't. Am I being strong and manly, or am I being banal? Why leave if it is only me crying, or is it the sound of her leaving? Or is it simply a gull crying? Who do I talk to in this staggering world when I feel like bawling? It is all so seminal.

Sometimes I feel like that little running rabbit with the shadow of the hawk between me and the glorious beauty of the sun.

Where does presence for me lie? It lies in this shinny silver-ringed glassy circle on my dashboard, my speedometer.

I push the gas pedal to the floor, and hope somewhere my peace will come. What will that be without you? Do I want it to be without you? What would that be?

I know you are there, so what? You are there, and when I am there with you, you are only (did I say only?), you are at me, clawing me, a she-cat at my guts. Is this why I am traveling?

Somewhere, cloths lie on the shivering floor. Somewhere, someone is rocking on her knees, traveling in a world of her own phantoms and doubts. What about him? Lonely, he is very lonely.

My tires smoke as I reverse gear out of my driveway. First gear, my tires scream and burn. Each journey, so goes the old saying, with the first step, mine begins with a blue cloud of rubber smoke that slowly drifts off to the east over my neighbor's house.

Cuda leaps as I jam the gas pedal, hitting the cattle guard at the end of our road, doing an even 100 miles per hour. Behind me on the gravel road a tornado of dust laid down flat, drifting off over the horses, cows, and pastures.

I am traveling away from love wreckage, is it totaled? Will there be love, joy, out the colored abstract blur now speeding by my fatigued car windows? My eyes are now my front door, the road my front yard.

Here on the cracked, sun-baked blacktop roads of Wyoming and the Yellow Stone country, my eyes hold yellow center lines, rusting railroad bridges, tiny deserted, sagging gas stations advertising Texaco gas. The rusty round Texaco signs, paint cracked and crazed, with a red star and a green T, offer fuel at 27 cents per gallon. The fuel nozzles are now homes for generations of spiders, hoping to fuel up on unwary flies.

Old barns, pastures, surrounded by zig zagging split-rail fences, come and go at 110 miles per hour. 75 miles down the country roads, I can't recall what barn was in what field, what copse of trees went with what river.

Small white houses with wind-time burnished siding stand in the shade of bent prairie trees. These trees forever, unceasingly bent with the continuous easterly winds. Occasionally, a barking dog. Sometimes a tall, rusting windmill, broken and stilled by time, blades hanging, bent like a plane crash.

Somewhere, set back in grasslands of grazing cattle, large red barns and small white farm houses. I race past, imagining a couple sleeping in their little warm and oh-so cozy double bed.

They sleep, spooned to each other, as the moon slides under old Grandfather's door. That pioneer door, its door jams are filled with all of the family history. Children ran in and out of that door, the dogs and soft brown puppies, one day a calf, born in the winter, carried in to be nursed by the warmth of the large old Round Oak Chief wood stove. Then, one day, Grandfather is carried out through that same door, never to return.

In some distant farm house out there on the prairie, as I listen in the center of my thoughts, someone sleeping, spooned, in love, makes unintelligible, sweet, gentle sounds that only contentment brings.

Large white barns, fenced with rails and barbed wire, have entrances framed by large clusters of standing varnished pine poles. Hanging over the miles long driveways are proudly carved signs, with ranch names like the "6666 Ranch", the "Rosewood Ramble", the "Chief Joseph" Ranch", the "Triple Creek" and "God's Little Acre".

Meandering rivers and creeks, 70,000 years old, formed on the Pitchstone plateau, that for endless eons had no names.

How ancient are our words? It strikes me that certain words are the same all over the world. I think of "Mama."

How much can I expect from life unfolding as I travel in it?

One stands alone on Bear Paw Mountain, holding aloft trembling iconic symbols of trees, buffalo skulls, turtle rattles. Do we know when we are symbols and icons? Are we the same as the cloud smeared sky? Is the moon more God than I?

My own time on this earth worms its way into my thoughts as my car starts to float at 130 miles per hour. I could run into a badger or coyote at this speed, and we would, most likely, even though born at different times, die together.

With this thought rummaging around my heavy foot on my gas pedal, I notice that at 130 the left front wheels starts to develop, only subtlety (after all I had these tires balanced last week), a nasty little disturbing rapid vibration. This vibration works its way into my thoughts as I watch antelope race across my rear view mirror.

Will their hooves etch the Pitchstone, and do we know if love will etch stone and our heart just as well? And while I am out here under this brilliant sun, I wonder, does shadow cause wear? The antelopes, the color of the scrub prairie grasses, disappear from my rear view mirror.

Lying beside me in my car are dried candies, coffee, dried up in squashed papers cups, a receipt for a small pizza, a few moldy cherries in a crumpled plastic bag, which I will throw them out when I fuel up next, they are staining the floor mats. There is a bill, marked paid, for a table and a night for one, at the Old Yellow Stone Lodge. Traveling alone you don't need too damn much. You need a mind that you can control from time to time, then let the whole thing happen.

Stare, wonder, forget all questions and answers, it's ok. Shut off your phone.

No mail, no paper, no news, no radio, except, perhaps, Mozart, Bob Wills, and Ella. That's being alone, that's ok. Let yourself drift and listen, think about it, then sing about it.

Somedays you may smell burning grasses and resinous pine forests. If you listen carefully, when you do stop, try tuning out the popping of your blistering hot 426. Perhaps you will hear the pioneers favorites, the trilling meadowlarks and, if you fortunately stopped beside a cattail pond or creek, the thrilling yet piercing ascending screech of the red-winged blackbird.

Maybe sitting there off the main drag,

perhaps on a little dusty gravel road, you may hear a calf bawl for its mother, or the classic cry of the red shinned hawk.

Unbeknownst to you, he is the owner of whole valley you stopped in. This is his world. Maybe, if luck's with you, you will hear the high pitched eerie squeal of a bull elk. Such a tiny voice for such a massive creature.

And a wolf, if God is riding on your fortunate shoulders, you may hear the ancient trembling wavering howl of a timber wolf.

I love afternoons like this on the road, where it is only me and the world unfolding, expectations high around every bend in the road and river.

What to make of a single tree standing alone, its own forest of one, in a thousand of acres of sage and prairie. On this hill the solitary tree's bark is burnished by howling wolves on night's iced moon. The dark purple shadow of the tree, a moon dial, slowly traverses the frozen snow round the tree while distant galactic stars circle and arc in the glacial moonlit air.

In the 110 degree heat of summer, amber elk bugling songs of love, the great beasts rub velvet, while burnishing their horns and scratch ticks from their sides on this singular tree. No need to count the elk. Countless generations, each elk calf taught by its family this is the spot where you come to rub.

Caves, shaped by dynamite and road crews, dripping water on my windshield, come and go and come again, this time with cyclist. Braking violently at 80, swerving into the oncoming lane, I am able to go around them. I couldn't have stopped. That's the road. The road is meant to roll on, to speed on. High speeds require elevated awareness.

An old friend of mine says that after your ability to have sex goes, you still have acceleration, and that it feels almost as good. He drove a 58 Chevy convertible with a 600 horse Viper engine. "Feels almost as good," is the caveat here.

Screaming down the little far-less traveled roads are rivers with Indian names like the Tongue, the Bears Teeth and the famous Little Big Horn, where Custer lost his blonde locks. Then the Madison came and went, filled with trout, a flatboat, and the occasional fisherman in boots.

Fly rod in hand, the fisherman thrashes the silver surface of the Madison, catching old trout with names like Buster and Old Silversides and Clip Fin that every guide knows. They have been caught many times before. Into the net, then held out to the camera to make them look larger, then gently put back into the river to be caught another day. Do you ever think, looking at a pretty woman in a red dress, or a man in a suave suit, "If I were a trout, I would be hooked."?

I am looking for answers to questions that I can't formulate.

Lonely is something we can all taste. It taste like tears, its breath is desire and cloying, its face is puffy, its neck is a grey landslide, it is alway worse at night.

We can try to ignore it by running ahead of these specters. Run, keep running, run until you can't breath, run until you cough up blood, but somewhere you will, you must, stop. There, lying on your side, your eyes at the level of the good earth, when you crack open your crusty tear-filled eyes, your demons will still be there, dancing their maniacal jig.

This is what experience tells me, though I try not to believe it, and so I run. Sometime I will stop, maybe you will be there, who ever you are. And when I stop, if you are there, who are you?

How much acceleration does it take to still the weeping? How fast must I, can I, drive to flee my thoughts?

What will I say to whomever when I get to wherever?

I have learned through much pain that there is never time for an explanation, that no one cares to hear my discord, they have their own pain. Everyone is in pain, be kind.

When my needs are said out loud, there is only my own echoing silence. Fearing that, when I try to explain through my veil of hurt and devastation, I will be left alone. There will be no harmony, not yet anyway. Sour grapes? Try it yourself.

No one, it seems, can see our world through our lamentations. With anguish and impossible hope, we pick up the cold phone, stare at its little glowing buttons, seeking, urging it to ring. It doesn't. On the road, silence your phone, put it in the trunk.

There is the crushing reality of leaving, forever, its myriad forms, its distortions, its

isolating macabre dances, faceless, endless-
ness without end.

The distances unknown and unreck-
oned. There is a face-sawing wind as I roll
down the window to clear my mind and
look out.

Running, tumbling sideways through
my sometimes receptive mind, my thoughts
are overwhelmed.

Sitting here, the 426, harshly gulping
at idle, shaking the Cuda, my thoughts, my
inner eyes, falling on recognizable shapes
and remembrances, then sliding into thick
fogs of unrecognition.

Forms skitter and press my thoughts
on the insides of my brain like a migraine,
causing obliterating pain and distortion.
Like most thoughts and some forms they
arrive uniquely.

My girl, my purple haired Cuda, with
her 426 throbbing heart, is my ticket to travel, to roll on. Her 426 is like the engine of my

mind, I must be open, all cylinders maxed, carburetion finely tuned, and from time to time open up my mind and burn out the carbon.

This requires, demands, that I have exquisite patience.

As it all reveals itself, I am left with this, a panoply so rich that I must write of it. Otherwise, without it, I will be like a plane without a vertical stabilizer.

This will all be in the chopper of last week's thoughts, hash, like last week's receipts for food that I don't remember ordering, and don't remember eating. Patience on the road is way more than talk.

There are signs, secret signs, be alert, rise, float, look down at yourself as you travel, be above the road, be aware of yourself and your surroundings.

Without solitude how can we discover our own voice? We are instruments out of tune, without timing and time alone. Out of time, out of sync, out of gear, out of gas, out, out, out!

Without the mental metronome, our timing is history.

Off by an inch, off by a mile.

Regrets? Yes I have a few.

The common element, the leitmotif of the road, is movement. Be lonely, keep moving, stop often.

Learn to laugh internally, let your spirit in, allow access.

Travel is about going and coming. Vital, if you desire it, is finding one's way back. Step out, go somewhere, you don't have to go a long way away to get away. As you travel you will know when to stop. We all need rest, food, and love. Sometimes, when you stop in the wrong place, perhaps in front of the wrong person or place, you will know. Look carefully, listen to your thoughts. Explore your mind, you will know. Be honest, be true to yourself.

If not true to yourself, then to whom? If not now, when?

It will soon be apparent, in this place where you stop, that there is not growth for you. That in this place you can live, but that is not the true essence of growth.

Scrub prairie grass lives a long life. Sagebrush plants, which talk with each other, live for over 100 years. Lichens cling to tectonic basalt columns, and have since Precambrian time. They are alive, as they slowly have been for 1.7 million years. The lifespan of a man or woman, a blink. "Start seeing everything as God."

The essence of life is the expression beauty.

What is life without you? Am I one, or am I two? Can I be one and survive, or must I be two? I think two, what an impossible choice. If sagebrush can talk to one another, why can't I talk to you?

When I am alone I feel as though I

am standing outside the world's window, watching an eternity away as a family plays. Is there no stasis, or, like the shark, must I keep moving to survive?

Someone in that world steps to the window, and lets down each shade at a time until the world around me grows dark. There are only slits around the windows of time.

As the slits around the edge of time darken, each light in the world is put out until the moon, our Luna, that other world, lights my face, and as I look up, I don't know what I feel like. Past my opal moon, a soft Great Horned owl flies on quivering loves wings.

I want to be 50 miles down this road before I need to have that thought again.

People all over the world let down shades, shut off all their lights.

I stand in the fresh cool prairie darkness, lit by stars, with a thousand luminous secrets, the answers to which I can only guess at.

At night on the Yellow Stone, stars make a mockery of a solitary man's time.

Alone under the great deep purple dome, stars cut from tessellated galactic patterns, glistening while I am curled in my old Hudson Bay four point blanket, my treasure in my vibrant beaded dreams. I dream on, as the moon rises, the earth rolling down. Somewhere, someone undresses.

At night it seems lonelier with the great stage curtain of heaven drawn up from the approaching night. This singular spot, on this deserted prairie, is where, tonight, I am playing out my life.

It is in this moonlight, ladled over the dry lands, that there comes to mind the desire to know. To know that what you really mean about warmth is kindness with sensuality.

A feeling of love, respect, kindness, and caring. Perhaps to massage each other, to try to bury, to detach from old restraints, and see if what we first saw in each other is still there.

Can we delight, inform, without prejudice, take chances on love, and believe we can make this work? Some days it seems that without you I can go on, and then some days I know I can't.

It may be, or more probably will be, that where you stop there will be restlessness, longing, thirst, loneliness, the dead, and newborns.

Wherever you are it will be the old world yet. It has been said before, of course, but you must be the change you want in your life.

Out here on the Yellow Stone, you might hear upright, still living pioneer pianos playing distant echoes from dead miners graves.

The piano, perhaps carried from "Ole Virginny" in a covered wagon, the family rocker, the old iron stove, heavy old precious objects, irreplaceable, so was the thought when they left the east.

Now these precious objects lie, sit, stand abandoned alongside the long winding dusty path west.

Granny too, maybe Grandpa, a newborn, maybe an arm, severed in an accident, also lie buried.

Maybe a frantic young mother searching for her lost child during a dust storm lies, where she fell, utterly lost, slowly buried by drifting sand in some nameless place near nameless buffalo bones.

Look carefully in abandoned ghost towns, and you will see sunken cellars where the miners' shacks once stood. Maybe at the bottom of a cellar, shards of purple glass, and, perhaps if luck's with you, a whole purple canning jar.

Pioneer cemeteries, with sunken graves, tell their own stories. They tell of the search for gold, which came up busted. Here in this place miners ached and fought, shot and shouted, picked and sluiced. Looking again for the third time as they swirl mud in the mining pan, squinting, and what did they get? More mud. There, lying off the old, overgrown road, the bones of a mule, alongside it, a rusting pick.

Spring rains, then summer droughts, then head high snows, and more empty mining pans.

A very few make a pile. One night the town burns.

Coyotes, looking down at the burning inferno, point their noses skyward to the smoky moon and howl. The light frozen wind takes away the icy vapor of their songs.

On the road there is time to think, or not think. Hungry, I eat. Thirsty, I drink. Sleepy, I sleep. Golden high prairies of vastness roll on, my dreams run out to meet them.

Here a dark blue and teal reflecting pond, reeds standing on the edge of its glittering, wind-ruffled waters, marsh hawks, hovering on flitting red wings, call, while over there, a mountain to climb.

Tucked away in a small pond in a field of cut tan wheat, four feeding black and white avocets. Through my telephoto lens I see their eager dark eyes, reverse curved bills probing the pond's rich mud, they dart and jerk.

I am restored once again, brought to tears. I cry easily on the road, alone, there is no place, and no need to hide my sorrow. Did I leave or did she?

The road stretches my mind. Over distant rolling hills, gray bent brooms of rainbow flecked rain sweep the land clean. Next, my Cuda is awash in hammering rains, then just as suddenly, sunny steaming wet asphalt.

At times, with my windows up, seat

heater on, I am hot. Then, with the rain stopping, down goes the window, out goes my hand to become a bird or plane. My flying hand becomes free of my arm, an extension of my floating thoughts.

Traveling alone is about the trip. It's a place where there is no one else but you, sky above and the good earth below. That is traveling alone. You don't need much, and you sure as hell don't need to know where you will eat or sleep that night. If you already know where you are stopping, why go? Traveling is about discovery. Don't spoil it by research, just go.

As the French writer, Jean-Paul Sartre noted, "Existence precedes essence," that only by existing and acting a certain way do we give meaning to our lives. We must invent our purpose, our own essence.

"Is this why I am traveling alone?" I ask myself.

Sartre also noted wryly, "If you are

lonely when you're alone, you are in bad company."

I stop at a small stone shrine beside a nearly deserted desert track on my way to a small ghost town that was who knows where, I sure as hell didn't, and I didn't know how far.

The small ancient dusty track is really too narrow for my car, which is being scratched by sagebrush.

This humble little shrine is surrounded by encroaching sagebrush and ragged hummocks of tall blue bending grass. On one bending stalk of grass, a meadow lark, a weather vane in the wind. The hot whipping desert wind blows steadily, ruffling my hair. Max, my little tan wire-haired terrier, explores.

In this far distant desert, standing alone on a low hill, overlooking a meandering river far below filled with quaking aspens, I find the shrine of "Jesus on the Cross".

He wears a crown of brown bramble thorns, his grimacing face and head are torqued, tortured, and pulled back in pain and wind sanded anguish. His blank eyes stare at the cloudless turquoise sky.

In one eye socket a spider has made its home. Blood runs down, always down, from the wounds from his piercing crown of thorns.

Blood runs into his face, dripping from his chin. His body, pierced in several places as well, has rivulets of now very pale blood. At his feet are clusters of now faded red plastic roses. The roses are only somewhat red at their core, while their edges are white plastic.

The drooping Jesus, hanging by the nails through his palms, is protected in his little stone shrine that at one time was limed and white. Now he is chipped and sanded by ceaseless desert winds, grey cement showing in cracked, tessellated patterns beneath the limed paint. Jesus, though still bloodied, is white as winter's driven snow.

In Jesus' outstretched hand he holds a faded red human-looking heart with a cross protruding from its top, surrounded by flames.

The heart has a bezel of thorns, with a dripping, bloodied, suppurated looking wound. Centered in the wound is a broken spear. The spear has been broken off long ago.

Nearby is a small sagging table, a place to sit. A place to think.

I am on the road. On the road, no one asks me questions. I want answers, and answers take questions.

Sitting there, I look out past a crumbled, twisted-board cattle shoot surrounded by a fence that has failed. Beyond the cattle shoot, surrounded by barbed wire, stands an old pioneer log cabin. Its roof long gone, the insides fill with snow each winter.

Nailed to the door, hanging by one hinge, a weathered sign: "STAY OUT, PRIVATE PROPERTY." I walk up and look in.

An old crushed rusted stove, a tangle that was once a bed, where perhaps lovers slept in each other's arms. I can't help saying that about the lovers, it's what I see. Two ghosts, nestled under a handmade quilt, a fire in the stove, banked for the night. Maybe out here, banked with buffalo chips.

Beside the bed, the remains of a piano, its black and still startling white keys silenced by the great smashing thumb of time and gravity.

As I walk around and look in at a crazily distorted side window, it occurs to me that just the other side of this blind present moment lies my creation, or someone else's. Much as I don't want to think about it, this is a death scene. Someone else's dream died here.

Was it also perhaps a destitute miner, dressed in his Sunday best, sitting on his bed on one useless Sunday, his shotgun in his mouth, his bare toe on the trigger?

You see, travel does that. Done right, it brings with it its own narrative.

It occurs to me that there is no place to hide on these plains, where farms look like antiques. Where there is weathered and wind-blasted steel confetti.

Old steel plows, a car, all four wheels in the air, harrows, twisted, destroyed, galvanized steel buildings drift in their own geologic way.

Out behind the house is a leaning cross, a wooden board grave marker where the inscription is too old to be read. Behind it, a sunken depression, a sage hen's nest. It flies up when I look in.

I also thought that simply being human, there is no place for me, like the sage hen, to hide either, on this oh-so confusing road of life. I feel some gigantic face looking down at me.

Walking back through the sage and scraggly desert grass to my car, I pull out an ice chest and carry it to the weathered sagging grey table.

The table, alive to my weight, groans as I set down the chest and sit along side it on top of the table.

Looking into the cool white interior of the chest, I find Italian hard sausage, a crusty baguette, hard cheese, tangy greek olives, small tart green gherkins, grapes, and a little dried prosciutto.

In the bottom, by some miracle, a 1998 bottle of Priorat, Clos De L'Obac, and a new hunting knife I had bought at a trading post with a beaded Indian sheath.

This a major meal, a minor miracle. As I pull the cork, the hot whistling winds pull and roll back the pages of my diary. The wind tips over my olive jar. Olives start rolling, the juice runs down into the cracks in the old grey table.

I dine alfresco, cutting the sausage, and baguette with my new knife, making tiny petit fours. A fill my apple-green stem glass, which I had purchased many miles ago, with the Clos De L'Obac. I savor its goodness.

I look at Jesus, standing for eternity nearby, still staring sightless into the sky. I raise my glass to his sky and toast him.

As I toast Jesus, I remember a vintner I met in Catalunya, Spain. Carlos Prostrada, who told me he could tell by the taste of his wines if there had been a rainbow as a burrow had walked up the mountain on the morning the grapes were harvested. I think I can taste the multihued rainbow.

Travel does this to you. You must go to adventure. It waits, like your dog wanting to go for a walk, but it won't come to you. For that matter, neither will your dog.

As the pages of my diary roll back, so does time, and before I can stop this descending time, it's her again, knees pulled up, and me the little running rabbit.

We must teach ourselves to hear our own voices. Who are we in love, and in lost love and alone? There is the metallic taste on our tongues. There is that gagging feeling that dissolves in morsels of hunger where we ravenously desire to eat our own heart. The soul-searing, metastatic, expanding growth of doubt. Soon, like some horrid disease it consumes and kills us. The taste of blood in our mouths, our desire to cry, "Are you there?" Blindly holding out our quaking hand, please someone take hold.

You see, on the road of life, everything seems to be going 100 miles per hour. How can we get a grip on life as it roars around and past us?

Like standing on the taffrail of a ship, the turbulent wake recedes as we are irrevocably carried forward and backward, away forever. Our distant thoughts, as confused as the turbulent wake, disappear into the offshore mists.

Is it that life is all going 100 miles per hour, or is it just illusion? Is zero the beginning, or is zero the end, or is it zero to infinity? "Zero is where the real fun starts, there's too much counting everywhere else!"

I shut the diary, putting a softball sized rock on it to silence its shouting monologue.

I drink my red wine with joy and gratefulness. While finishing my lunch, I watch as yellow jackets lunch on the dead bugs smashed in the grill of my Cuda.

Packing up my luncheon on the table I get into the Cuda, turn the little silver key, igniting its eight cylinders. I drive away from the still staring wind-sanded Jesus.

Driving away, the yellow jackets fly with me until at 15 miles per hour they give up.

It all looks so simple from inside my car, those distant prairies. Stone layers of twisted sea bed, bent and filled with nektonic swimming fish in ossified oceans. Nature looks so serene, so elegant, so perfect in its gigantic volumes. Nature is so complicated, and it occurs to me that I am also part of nature.

My life is complicated. Not as complicated as any ordinary rock face I race past, but to me, yes, complicated.

Arriving back at the pavement, I look down at the passenger side floor mat. It looks like a scrambled egg once again. Traveling, I don't fight it, I accumulate. There are rocks and feathers, new and old books, photographs of pioneers from antique shops. I like to nose around in small town antique shops. When I travel I try to find one glass that I use on the road and also take into restaurants with me. My antique apple-green stem glass is just such a purchase.

There is somewhere in that strata of objects, on the passenger side floor, a two hundred year old buffalo skull, from the bottom of an ancient Indian buffalo cliff. The early Indians drove buffalo off these cliffs by the thousands, butchering them where they fell to their deaths, trilobites ossified to stone.

Somewhere, crushed, more paper cups with dried frappuccino, sage lip balm from an Indian trading post, sweet grass bundles, an old white native-beaded bag, black bananas, peanut shells, tissue, both used and not, and finally a 100 year old lithograph of an owl, Tyto Alba Guttata, that seems to want to fly away each time I open my rear door.

Somewhere from time to time I find my reading glasses, my sun glasses, and my distance glasses.

I am a long way from home and I can say easily I am not organized.

All I want, simple as Old Faithful, is

love.

I am looking for that love in farmlands, rangelands filled with cattle and horses, rivers so innocent, filled with life, that I am brought to tears once more.

Hills, the grey color and rolling shape of a Shar Pei, slide by my bug splattered windows. Do I find love out there in that prairie? Absolutely yes. A woman's love? No.

I roll on, 115 is the right speed for the Cuda, no wheel vibrations, no strange sounds, the engine purring like the tiger she is. What a sound, nothing like it, the rolling throaty magnificence of a titanic 426 V-8.

Somewhere between 110 and 120 is meow, purrs like a kitten.

Feed her the right high-octane sweet cream, troubles are history.

I can and do pass everything on the road, except rabbits and coyotes, at right angles. What was that thud?

Flying at 122 miles per hour, I come up on my right side to a seemingly endless freight train racing me side by side. It roars, rattling, its screeching, squealing wheels shake the ground. Pulling past 100 cars, I finally come even with five power-filled invincible diesel engines. Jet blasts of heated grey-black smoke flood the pure turquoise prairie sky. Easing off the gas, I drift back.

Graffiti smeared box cars, doors closed and stamped with "Great Northern."

Interspersed with empty shells of coal cars open to the sky, an oil tanker. They all clatter along.

I roll down my windows to hear this industrial monster better, small bits of paper (my receipts?) fly out my open window. As the freight goes over, I go under at a bridge.

Just before I go under the railroad bridge, I see an old black man standing in one of the open coal cars, waving. I wave back. Maybe I buy him dinner and a beer in a small diner in some cow town, I fantasize.

How often on the road of life do we meet someone on a sidewalk and think, in barely a nano second glance as they walk toward us, "Had we but world enough and time, this coyness, lady, were no crime. We would sit down, and think which way to walk, and pass our long love's day," but then we walk on by.

In a small cowboy bar a beautiful waitress, lips closed, coyly smiles. I smile back. I try to say something sweet, enduring. I say, "Everywhere you and you alone in secret fields of gold." She laughs, has no front teeth. I think that, "Not for ourselves alone are we born," pay the bill. It won't be this woman.

Stepping out into the gravel parking lot, I see the distant sheet lightning of an approaching storm. Jagged night neon forks of more lightning dance on little mountains. These little prehistoric mountains feel, be-

fore the wind and blue sky, the dream se-
quence.

Hammered gold, the moon shines on a
golden pond. I am moving through at 100
miles per hour, and with windows down,
the evening breezes fill, perfuming my car
with hay and cattle.

Stick with me on this, but I am pretty
sure, after a couple shots of Jack, I think it
was a couple, might have been three, and
two beers, go figure, anyway I thought that
I heard a chorus of frogs, and I still wonder, but I swear they saluted as I drove by.
But listen, I am not going to hang my hat on
this. It is only this, that when you are alone
you see and hear things that you might not
otherwise hear or see. Being alone shouldn't
be about what we will be someday, but this
day. Traveling alone is about the trip, it's a
place where there is no one but you.

It's your game, see and feel whatever
you want.

What is this God thing, passion, this narrow road strewn with oh-so pretty blossoms?

Last night was potential torture as I got caught in rapidly falling darkness. No lights, only the occasional glaring vaporous barn light. Sometimes a distant farm light down a long driveway, rolls of bailed hay illuminated in my headlights. I am a long way down this road when I see a shot up sign that says, "Next services 50 miles." My parched Cuda, sucking at the dregs in my capacious fuel tank, slowly rolled into a small one-horse town, the horses long in bed, with one very hermetically sealed, closed Sinclair gas station, no motel, no cafe, even the barking dogs had crawled under their porches. All is quiet, there is the iconic occasional front porch light, a small dim light in some upstairs window, otherwise, dark and peaceful. Unless you are looking for a place to fuel up and a place to sleep, then anxiety.

I think, "I am SOL," when I notice a little white sign nailed to a power pole, advertising overnight borders welcome. "Bobcat Lodge."

An arrow on the sign, an address with a rural route number, two miles, "Welcome Bob Jr. and Marcie Wills." A telephone number, I call. "Y'all come on up," a wide awake man's voice intones. "Large white house on the right, two miles on the gravel, I'll turn on the porch lights for ya." A life line.

I hang up, mutter to myself, "Thank you, Jesus."

I see the porch light, half a mile away across cut hay fields. Another sign in the head lights, "Open rangeland, watch for cattle on the road." As I near the house, I start to see large lumps of manure in the gravel road. Soon a cow shows up in my head lights, then two, then a whole herd standing alongside the gravel road, and in the road itself.

Gingerly nosing through the herd, they calmly walk out of my way, swishing their tails, with the occasional cow bucking and running off wildly into the field beside the road. Stopping in the middle of the herd, I shut off my heated engine while rolling down my windows. Their great brown eyes reflect in my headlights. Some bawl a soulful moan, others grunt, some groan. One curious cow, with a whiskered wet pink nose, puts his face into my window. I give him my last carrot. He walks off, and then, tuned to some signal, they all in mass start to bawl, as though taking to each other. I crank the 426. They all jerk, and move off into the fields, leaving me alone on the manure-splattered dusty road. I drive on.

Turning through the sagging arch over the driveway, I see a hanging sign: "Bobcat Lodge, Bob Jr. & Marcie Wills." Slowly driving up a half mile long row of poplar trees I come to an old white farm house. As I shut down the engine, I see a large cat run across the porch. I mean a large cat, not a house cat. Max sees it too, and growls.

Just when I wonder if I should open the door, a man comes out of the house, yells out to me in the dim dark yard light, "It's ok, he is on a chain."

I yell back, "I have a dog."

"Leav'im in your car til later," he shouts back.

Walking up to the old sagging porch, he puts the cat behind him and opens the front door for me. Once inside, I notice it is decorated, varnished, clean, with guitars hanging here and there, new and old.

"Welcome, how can I be of help?"

"Do you have a room for the night?" I ask, inwardly praying the answer is yes. It's either here or my back seat.

"Well now, that depends," he says.

I wasn't expecting that. "What do you

mean?" I queried.

"Pretty simple," he says. "It depends on whether I like you or not."

I think about that for a moment, then say, "How are we to determine that?"

"Well," he says, "I kind of already think you're ok, since I like people with dogs. Scotch drinker?" he asks.

"I'm Scot, Isle of Skye," I say.

"Come on in by the fireplace, I was just sitting down with one. I collect Scotch, not Scots," he chuckles, a kind of cigarette chuckle at his own joke. "I like you even better. Now, if you was one of them teeto-taler or a Mormon, well, bets are off..." he trails off chuckling. "Low land, highland, peat, no peat, whatever you like I probably have it."

"Well, hum, quite a question," I think. I like this guy more and more. "How about The Low Flying Bird or Dalmore single malt or," I was warming to the subject now, "don't s'pose you have Glenmorangie Signet, by some rare chance?"

At that he gets up, throws a couple of large logs on the fire, then turns and says, "What are you, some kind of a goddamn wizard?"

Shocked by his tone, I think I might be sleeping in the back seat yet, when he pipes up and says, "Well, 'cause I just poured a Glenmorangie Signet, just before you and your dog pulled up." Turning he walks over to an old liquor cabinet made of weathered barn boards with large rusty hinges. He fiddles with glasses and bottles over there with his back to me as I look at the large rustic room.

Navajo blankets, a gigantic chandelier made of elk horns, baskets, woven and intricate, tanned cow hides on dark worn fir floors. A grand piano, which I make out to be a Bluthner, with five or six guitars in stands standing nearby.

I also notice a microphone on a tall chrome stand. Just as he turns to me, and in an infectious way says, "Knowing you the little I do, no ice I am sure, and here is a dropper for a few drops of pure mountain spring water, for your scotch. I get this water from a little trickle that filters from a ancient basalt formation up in the painted hills where I hunt. Only use it in my Scotch, pure as angels tears."

"Cigar?" he asks.

"How did you know?" I respond.

"Just a lucky guess," he says, smiling. Reaching into a small leather colored mahogany humidor on the table by his maroon leather chair, he opens it and lifts out two elegant Davidoff Winston Churchills. He sets a gold embossed ashtray on my side table, which was made of plow disk, hammered flat.

Then, handing me a cutter and a box of wood matches, he settles himself back in his chair, feet out toward the roaring fire. He cuts the end of his cigar, lights it, draws on the cigar, and blows the smoke into his scotch.

On my match box it says, "Crillon Hotel, Paris, France."

"Cheers," he says. We touch our cut glass snifters. I hear that pleasing musical ping of crystal glass.

He rolls his cigar around and around in his large hand in silence for a moment, and then, taking a full puff, blows it out into the fireplace, saying, "This was the only cigar my father ever smoked."

"A man of taste," I say.

"You may have heard of him," he says.

"Probably not," I say. "I'm not from these parts, or anywhere near here."

"Bob Wills was his name," he says. "Bob Wills and the Texas Playboys."

I sit straight up, coughing. "Bob Wills was your father?" I choke out.

"Damn straight," he says.

"What a pleasure to meet you. King of the Western Swing," I say.

"I remember my dad use to love his music, danced my mother all over our little living room. Faded Rose, Sugar Moon, My Little Cherokee Maiden."

"Damn," I say, "this takes me back. I remember dad use to also dance with mom, Waltz Across Texas. Hell, they sure don't make 'em today like they did in your dad's time."

At that he gets up and goes over to pick up an old Gibson steel stringed guitar, and sits back down, balancing the guitar on his knee, and begins to play John Conlee's Rose Colored Glasses.

Tears come to my eyes. What a bitch, happy one moment, aching the next from deep hurts buried just beneath the surface of this bag of skin I live in.

Finishing the song, noticing my tears, he says, "Finish that scotch, and I'll make you one of my specialities, elk steak with morels. Marcy went to bed early, they're out gathering wild onions tomorrow morning at the break of dawn. I will be doing the cooking for us, which I do 95% of the time anyway. Not a burden though, since I was taught to cook way back by my mother, dad as well, when he wasn't on the road. It's just another form of creation.

No different than playing the guitar, singing, dancing, painting, or hunting."

As Bob jr, heads out to the kitchen, I sit there in the warmth of the fireplace, enjoying the pitchy pine smoke of the fire, sipping the scotch, thinking I have a place to sleep.

"Life is funny that way," I think. Seems like when I am the happiest, around the corner comes a freight train of grief. Where is the balance, or is that the balance? I don't think I understand life, never have really. I only know that a poet once said,

"Everyone once, once only. Just once and no more. And we also once, never again. But this having been once, although only once, to have been of the earth, seems irrevocable."

We, alone, own our histories, that can't be taken from us.

Seems to me we are like those conglomerate rocks. Conglomerates are made up of hundreds of different kinds rocks, of all shapes and colors. Pressed together in one matrix.

Here a granite, there a jasper, here a jade, endless variations, a myriad of small, finely ground bits of sands and crystals. Well, you get the idea, all kinds of diverse rocks pressed into one big whole ball. Cut a conglomerate open and you get jagged edged rock, smooth big and small boulders, all dissimilar, in color and shape.

It occurs to me that inside each of us are little endless myriads, dark and light fleshy conglomerates. Dark pockets where we broke a wrist, killed an owl for which we are forever pained, left a good woman. Migraines lie in wait in remembrance of that event in your life. You performed some monstrosity of deceit, perhaps this deceit destroys your upper back between your shoulder blades when you think or remember it. Mental and physical sprains dance and sing for joy at hurts we can't control.

Fleshy conglomerates are in each of us, some smooth and soothing, others sharp and painful. They are scattered around our whole being, our thoughts and our physical selves.

Our minds and bodies have memory, coiled steel springs of waiting grief and joy. That warm, reassuring joy of a nursing child, the warm joy of being nursed. There is the pain of a circumcision, the seminal, indescribable feeling of climax.

That rotator cuff you thought was healed and gone for ever crouches, waiting. That broken wrist still hurts if you abuse it. You thought it was healed.

Here, there, scattered like malicious abusive demons. Your divorce lives in the muscles at the back of your neck, your hurt at being told by an abusive teacher you couldn't paint lives in your shoulder, ever so subtly, when you try to paint, radiating down your arm. The hostile message that you are less than lives in your lower back.

It is all in there, the pure infant that we were at the moment of birth. We barely slide past the pelvic tunnel when we hear the grunting crying of our mothers, the screaming no longer muted by the protective placenta. We are pushed out, ejected, until we are finally out of the warm, moist security of the womb. The cold air rushes in and then, with no ceremony, we are forced out, lifted by our feet into the dry hostile world and slapped.

Does that slap stay with us? Is it our first lesson?

Memory doesn't just occur in our cerebral grey matter, it exists all through our bodies. Memory is everywhere throughout us. It lives in our guts, bones, thoughts, randomly scattered joy and pain. Is it random?

As we get older we need to perhaps be a little more cautious, yet who wants that? More pain, more joy, more memories, live free. Caged or uncaged, for me no gilded cage. Give me freedom, or give me death. Or the chance to fight for my freedom.

Infinity is boundless. Get use to no fences, because that is where you are heading, your greatest road trip.

Staring fixedly into the space between me and the fire which is slowly, heatedly collapsing, I think of her, I think of me. Eroding my mental barriers, looking for absolution, I'm not yet finding it.

Then someone, in a place as far down a cow filled gravel road as the Bobcat Lodge, out on a 70,000 year old plateau in Montana, where coyotes polish the night skies, under a rolling, arcing moon, and who shows up? How far, how fast do I have to drive to get away?

I know the answer, please say nothing.

Here is a guy, in the most random of situations, that I don't know from Adam singing and playing Rose Colored Glasses, and the pain wells up like a super-heated puss-filled boil.

My eyes fill, I am smoking a great cigar, drinking superb single malt, happiness like a blanket.

Then I jump, tears a ball in my throat, a sob barely controlled, my mouth's memory remembered. Because my tattletale mouth is so exaggeratedly contorted, my host, thank you sir, pretends not to notice and chooses at that moment to do a close study of his cigar. He holds it out, examining it, pulls it in, places it between his warm, pliable lips, takes a puff, looks at the clock, all the while as I struggle to gain control of the shock of that instant.

As Bob sings and plays those few musical bars from John Conlee's Rose Colored Glasses, the words seem to me to be the magic bullet for the target of my grief.

How could I be so afflicted?

"I don't know why I keep on believ'n you need me when you've proved so many times that it ain't true. And I can't find one good reason for stay'n, maybe by leave'n would be the best for you. But these rose colored glasses that I'm looking through show only the beauty, 'cause they hide all the truth."

Where was it crouching, hiding, just so vicious, these camouflaged assassins? I close my eyes for a moment, just a moment, and an ogre stares back. I need another scotch, maybe two.

My burdened mind tries to darkly take over, when just at the perfect moment, I begin to smell delicious fragrances coming from the large old lodge kitchen.

I go to the kitchen door and ask about the cat. "In bed in his kennel," my delightful host calls back. Walking out into the marvelous night air, covered with a star quilt, Max takes a pee and we go into the house.

He could cook, that son of Bob Wills. Sixteen ounce elk steaks, rare. I tell him that I had seen elk burnt worse than those steaks and survive. He laughs. With the elk came a subtly delicious rosemary scented brown gravy, sifted over with smashed lavender blossoms.

Along side the steaks are small wild onions with roots still on, along with their wilted green steamed stalks, dusted with sumac. There are small yellow al dente

Finnish potatoes from his garden that he boiled in shallow salted water with several handfuls of old dark dank-looking maple leaves from last year. I look at this and ask, "Tell me? Most unusual." I say.

He tells me it is an old family recipe from Upsala, Sweden, from his grandmother. He says, "The slightly decayed leaves advanced the earthiness of the potatoes, while the maple leaves gave the whole dish a woodsy bottom note."

We drink two bottles of Australian 2019 Coonawarra estate John Riddoch Cabernet Sauvignon in large tulip Ridell glasses. He set along side, and with the cabs, small cut crystal shot glasses of Eagle Rare, seventeen year old Kentucky bourbon whiskey.

We hover over our steaks with bone handled hand-forged steak knives, sharp as surgical instruments.

Let's see, we don't eat every second. In fact we talk a lot, but what we talk of who knows what. Pardon me, I totally forget, but I can tell you this: I am either mesmerized or very drunk. If I were betting on this, I would chose the latter.

With the steaks come small crunchy carrots, steamed and rolled in sesame seeds, then dusted with wasabi powder.

Varied greens from his garden, with small triangles of preserved lemon, with juice from the preserved lemon jar, and virgin olive oil from Sicily are the final touch after the full rich meal.

White wine, of course, a French Sancerre with the greens. "Greens are the broom of the bowl," he says, and laughs that same chuckling laugh.

I think, "I have been living in a cave. This very complexed individual made everything he touched look so simple, such genius."

What is it about genius? It all looks so simple, or as the saying goes, "Easy for

Leonardo."

What have I been eating? I can tell you again, but I have already told you ad nauseam. It is spread all over the passenger side floor of my Cuda, I'm not going to lintanize it for you except to say none of it was more than you could lift, and your grandmother would most likely not recognize any of the ingredients.

All the while, beginning with the moment I walked back into the kitchen with Max, we drink heavily. Which is, at this moment (that's the caveat: at this moment, but who knew about tomorrow. I am getting too drunk to really think about tomorrow, let alone about the whirlies in bed later.), perfect, or so I think.

After the double fire place scotches, my ever so delightful host, Mr. Wills Jr. by name, in the kitchen while he cooks, brought out a chilled bottle of Verve Clicquot, yellow label brute, and two crystal champagne glasses.

I wink, and said infectiously, laughing, "Bubbles, always before dinner, helps the medicine go down."

I will say this right up front, Mr. Wills Jr. only drinks, smokes, and eats the best, which from the little I know, he searches the world over for the best and most unique.

Normally when I travel, food is the binder. However, this road trip on the Yellow Stone, tears seem to be the glue.

Let me be as clear as I can at the moment. Ah clear, I can't be with the array of drink and food we have consumed. Then there is always the surprise of the unturned card, that old bugaboo women rummaging around in my body and mind, which doesn't lead to clarity either.

I can talk about whiskies, cigars, food, but goddamnit stay off the topic of women. Don't ask me about women, I am numb on this topic. Remember what I say, "Fleeing love wreckage."

If I said this before, forgive me, I don't like to repeat. In fact I hate to get caught repeating. The world's primarily a world of numbing consistency, and someone said it best, "Consistency is the hobgoblin of small minds." So I can talk on a variety of topics, pick one, just not women. At least not this drunken night.

We stumble back to the fireplace. Bob Jr. picks up his steel string, and plays blues riffs, sings a few ballads Bob Wills Sr. wrote, until I drift off, it has been a long day.

He gently nudges my foot, and as he does so he holds out a short blunt to me. As I put it to my lips, he torches it.

"I think the Roy Rogers suite is best for you, great king bed, its own patio, open to the mountain view and the purling Yellow Stone river, second door on the right."

I get up and fall right back down into the leather chair. "Maybe I will sleep here," I drunkenly murmur.

He says, "You will be more comfortable in a real bed," and as he walks me to the door I stumble against the varnished newel post leading to the upstairs rooms. "There you go, Buckeroo, Roy Roger suite is yours. Room number two, down the hall, straight ahead."

"How much for all of this, Bob?" I mumble.

He says, "It's free or not free. There is an empty goldfish bowl in the room, leave whatever you want inside the bowl, or don't, up to you." This was past my thinking ability at that moment.

"Great to meet you," Bob says. "Thanks for entertaining me tonight, it gets lonely out here. See you in the A.M. Get up whenever you feel like it."

The Roy Rodgers suite has a little dog bed with a Navajo style cover lying over by the French patio doors. Bending down, I show it to Max, pat it with my hand so he would jump in, and promptly fall on my face in the little dog bed. I get up, and fall against the wall. Max looks quizzically at me, then slowly, while giving me the eye, climbs into his little bed. While I climb back onto my feet, I put my hand against the wall, watching as Max turns round and round a half dozen times, scratches the bed thoroughly, roughs it all up, curls into a ball, puts his tail over his eyes, and sleeps.

I stumble to the bed, sit down heavily, and fall backwards across the bed onto my back on top of the western quilt, instantly passing out, the lights all still on.

Some indistinct drunken time later in the night, waking with the spinning room, one of those shouting voices asks, clearly and urgently, "Do you love me?" It is so loud that I look around the room for some-one.

Rolling over, now hideously awake, blinded by the light, cotton mouth assails me. I drink some water, pull back the cowboy sheet and covers, shut off the bedside light, crawl into the bed, laying my head gently on to the deliciously soft goose down pillow. Even though drunk, I still smell that wonderful reminiscent home fragrance of sheets and pillows that have been hung out to dry on an outdoor clothes line.

I drift back into nothing except jet black once more.

I am a long way from home and my turbulent dreams turn into nightmares.

My neighbor lady at home, whom I severely dislike for the way she treats her husband, children, and dog, came drifting over me, naked, crouching, holding a candle beneath her chin. Her sagging breasts are sallow, with protruding black nipples. I cringe. Who is this maniacal dark creature, climbing into my thoughts? This awful human being, this frighteningly spectral ghost dancing around me, filled with hate and loathing, shouting, "Do you love me?"

She stands over me, high above me, a leg on each side, and tries to push her black oily bush in my face. My soul shrinks. This goes on, she smiles, laughs, shouts, her breath awful. I open my eyes, yelling, "Get away!" and find Max on the bed with a worried look, licking my face. She, the dark neighbor, vanishes. I grab Max for comfort, pulling him to me, then slide once more into restless sleep.

The little air conditioner pleads, it shuts off, then on, then off, then on. Regardless, I am still hot and sweaty, I need more water. I wake myself up, take a glass into the big bathroom, swill down three glasses of water, then head back to bed. I roll over on my side, putting my hands between my drawn up knees, and pass out again.

I hear her coming. This time it is the beautiful waitress with rotted front teeth from some cafe somewhere back on the road.

She glares, shrieks in laughter when she sees I recognize her, her breath is green, fetid, vaporous. She seems to feel that I recognize her is hilarious. Then, while standing in the middle of someone else's bedroom, she rips off her jeans and panties, then reaching behind her back, she undoes her black bra, letting her bountiful shapely breasts free. She advances on me, reaching under the covers at my crotch. I cower under my dreams.

Max whines. I am back awake. The waitress, thanks to Max, is gone. Getting up, I open the patio door, stepping out into the cool, refreshing night air. Max walks off the porch and pees.

Somewhere a coyote howls. A dog barks in response. A light, refreshing breeze flows over my sweaty body. How long have I been rolling, turning, tossing in that bed?- Cattle, lots of cattle, bawl in the very early morning air. The dry air smells of cut hay fields, somewhere, a skunk. Far off on the horizon I can see the gentle soft orange of approaching day. A rooster crows, I hear the bobcat meow.

Looking up, I see a green shooting star. I am happy and smile, thinking, "I love the open road." I feel restored once more.

"Bob Wills Jr., what a unique individual," I think. You don't find people like him everyday, hardly any day. For him and people like him, enough is never enough. What a treat.

Calling to Max, we go back in to our Roy Rodgers suite. While climbing into my bed, Max jumps up on the bed beside me, and putting his head on my pillow, sighs a long sigh, nestles his head near mine, and is soon asleep. Lying back, my hands behind my head, I wonder what Dale Evans looks like in the nude, chuckle, and immediately fall into a deep, restful sleep.

Waking long after the prairie sun had

risen, I rise, lead back to awareness by the smell of fresh coffee drifting from the kitchen. Max and I walk out through the grand living room, the fireplace still smoldering, and on into the kitchen. Bob is at the table playing solitaire.

Looking up, he smiles, and says, "Coffee is on the stove, your breakfast is in the heating oven."

Looking at the chiming grandfather clock I see it is ten.

My head doesn't feel so good. He sees this and sets a cool beer by my side on the table, and while laughing says, "Hair of the Dog."

In a big kitchen chair the bobcat, with its magnificent reddish coat and subtle dark spots, lays sleeping, heedless to all of us, on its back.

Max sees the cat and jumps up into my lap. We both laugh. "Really," he says, "in the real meaning of the word, he is a pussy cat. He is tame and loving, just intimidating because of his size. He wouldn't harm a flea."

My breakfast of farm fresh eggs, over easy, Canadian bacon, fruit, buttermilk biscuits with fresh chokecherry jam on the side is restorative. I drink about a gallon of fresh cool spring water, no ice. I am starting to come around.

We sit for a while, talking about cattle, crops, the weather, the bobcat, nothing really of any real meaning. That is something else I like about Bob, you don't always have to be talking, often times silence says enough.

We are silent for a while, then he says, "I heard you moaning in your sleep last night."

I look quickly away at the brilliant blue sky out the farmhouse windows, where the sun is slanting in through the hazy, smokey air in the kitchen. The sun, landing on the old dark polished fir floors, reflects back up, making little patterns of light on the white leaded glass-covered kitchen cabinets.

I look back into the kitchen and manage to say, "This has been splendid," choking up, and again tears. Bob gets up to clean the dishes and pretends not to notice my obvious pain.

"Say," I finally ask, as I get myself back under control, "is the Sinclair gas station open? I don't even know what day this is."

"No", he says, "been closed for about five years. Need fuel?"

"Yes," I say.

"Pull over by the barn fuel tank when you are ready to leave, I will fill her up," he says.

"I left cash in the goldfish bowl, I hope it's enough, though I don't think I could leave you enough. What a meal, what drinks, but what I mean by saying that is I couldn't leave you enough. It's this, your company has been priceless."

He smiles, "It's enough."

Going out to the car, Max jumps in the passenger seat as I slide into my side behind the wheel. I ignite the 426 and drive over to the barn fuel tank where Bob is standing.

Getting out, Bob takes a nozzle and coiled hose off of a hook on the tank, while I open the fuel cap.

Looking the Cuda over, its grill filled with moths, yellow jackets, hornets, butter-flies, the hood bug-splattered, the whole car is dirty, dusty, and the windows are beyond streaked.

He offers, "Over on the side of the barn is a hose, a bucket, and car wash soap if you want to clean her up a bit, just saying. Pretty crumby for such a great looking machine."

Standing there he says, "Is that a stock color?"

"Ya," I say, "factory, plum crazy purple."

"What's the power plant?"

When you crank it up, it sounds pretty throaty. "426, dual four barrels, sucks a lot of fuel," I say.

"What's its top speed, do you think?"

"Well," I say, "I figured I had her topped out trying to catch a freight train the other day at right around 135 miles an hour. Scary at that speed though. The whole car starts to float, and an unseen dip in the road? Terrifying."

"Just so you know, not preaching here, but if you get caught by the highway patrol going 135, it's a felony. Kiss your license goodbye for years, if not forever, not to mention jail time. If you get stopped speeding anywhere in this county, call me," he says. "All the cops round here know me, I've been stopped a few times myself," he says, chuckling.

"Is there a bottom to this tank, or is fuel running out on the ground?" he laughs again. "How many miles to the gallon do you get?"

"Six on a good day," I say.

"What does it do in the quarter mile?"

"Zero to 60 in 5.8 seconds," I say.

"Are these cars expensive? Not that I could use it around here on the farm, I don't see a plow attachment," he kids.

"Well", I say, "on Mecum auction, I'm sure you have heard of them, a convertible, same color, same engine, sold for $3.5 million."

Getting out my wallet, I ask, "How much for the fuel?"

"Well now, that depends," he smiles.

"Depends?" I ask. "On what?"

"Here we go again," I think.

"Well, you don't see a gauge, do you?" I look. No gauge, just a nozzle, hose and a tank.

"So let's just say I am paying it forward," he says. "I won't charge you, just pay it forward to someone else you meet. Like I said last night, it gets a bit lonely out here. So if you come back up this road, stop in. You haven't had my Coq au vin yet, and I am positive I have scotches you haven't tried."

There comes that ball in my throat again. I can't seem to control the corners of my mouth around this wonderful man.

He helps me wash the windows, Bob Wills Jr., son of Bob Wills and the Texas Playboys, Kings of the Western Swing, while I wash the Cuda. "Will wonders never cease?" I think. He gives me a vacuum for the inside, and before I know it, my plum crazy Cuda is clean as a whistle, and I am on my way out the driveway. "That's the road," I think. Extend yourself, keep moving, stop often.

Once off the gravel and back on the small paved blacktop road I see a sign. I*dian res***vat*ion m*s*um, 7* *iles. The part of the sign that gives the name of the museum and its hours has been blasted by bullet holes to unreadability.

Goosing the Cuda over a 100 miles per hour to reach the museum against a time of which I had no knowledge, nor a distance, either, for that matter. Opened Closed? Who knew? I had no way of knowing. Some person, or persons, had used the sign for target practice.

Reaching the Indian museum, I found a shabby kind of government tan brick building, reminiscent of old military bases.

As I climb stiffly out of the heated Cuda, the wind is blowing very hard, banging a screen door somewhere. Small desiccated trees, low on water, struggle. Among the grey-tan grasses, a dandelion is flowering.

I heard that somewhere out there, that on the plains of Montana and Wyoming, the jet stream touches the earth.

As I drive up, a bus load of venerable

citizens stand around the entrance. One pretty younger black-haired Indian woman jerks on the ossified chicken-wire entrapped doors, even though a sign in the window shouts in red, "Closed for Remodeling, Join us in the spring for our grand opening."

They turn, shouting to each other while returning to their grey bus. Some of them attempt to light cigarettes in the wind. Their dejected, disappointed words, which I try to hear, are sent sailing down the desert wind on the wings of a passing meadow lark. I hear nothing, only I read from the parking lot, "Closed, return in the spring." I won't be waiting that long. In fact, I won't be waiting at all.

Opening the car door for Max, I take him around the back of the museum so he can pee.

Around back, there is high chainlink fence between the museum and endless desert. It's blowing so hard tumble weeds dance and roll, some coming to a stop insnared in the chain link fence.

As Max pees, I peer in the museum's dirty, chicken wire meshed back windows. I see vitreous congealed display cases containing ghost shirts, riddled with bullet holes.

As I walk along looking in other windows, I see spear points, beaded clothes, polychromatic beaded moccasins, old Hudson Bay four point blankets.

Walking along in the dry grass, peering in other windows, I see rifles, saddles, horse blankets and bridles.

In another glass case, I see in the dark, unlit interior knives, tomahawks, kettles and drums. These particular drums now silenced forever.

It occurs to me that museums are the last stop for many civilizations.

One example among thousands would be the great "Templo Mayor" in the Aztec capital of Tenochtitlan, now Mexico city, which lies buried under busy carbon-exhausted city streets. This ancient civilization only exists in museums today, and is vaguely, if at all, understood.

Precious objects have no defense, except what we, the living, give them. Sotheby's, the great delightful auction house in London, is the Heathrow of orphaned objects. From around the world bits and pieces of civilizations, families, and wars arrive. Arrive, and in a great dispersion, are gone. Do we own our rings and things, or do they own us? Unless we are buried with those rings and things, like Salvador Dali, the intensely creative Spanish artist, at his own choosing was buried in his Cadillac, limousine.

When we cease, our objects move on. Inanimate objects move on their own around the world everyday. You, me, pick them up, carry them, then drop them, sell them, forget them, bury them, they glacially, sometimes rapidly, move. In animate objects have legs.

How wondrous this, how mysterious!

I carry fuel, I draw water.

Walking up to the last window, I peer around the corner of the building just in time to see the grey senior bus pulling out into the street. Written on its side, in large white letters, "Seniors Living With Jesus." It's smoking diesel sends a cloud of black smoke, which rapidly dissipates on the gusting winds out over the pristine prairie.

I turn back to the building, peering into this last dirty corner window.

In this corner window I find a beautifully painted teepee. Clustered in front of it, a depressing dead diorama.

A wax family, mute, secluded, blank staring eyes, glaucoma, endlessly, eternally, forever. The young warriors, dusty and rigid, the women crouching, downcast, holding babies in papoose bindings, forever trapped. There are no elders.

There are in those glass eyes holding dusty blood of what once was, and would never be again. That train, as the saying goes, has left the station. It is important, however, to remember, as once happened to me, we may get on the wrong train and end up at the right station.

This was the wrong station, this very cheerless, woeful, sad boxed display cage, detritus.

I call Max, turning for the car, asking why I was so depressed by what I saw.

Getting back in the car, I feel that lump in my throat again. Turning the key in the dash of my plum crazy purple Cuda, my war horse, I think any warrior would kill, or steal, to get a purple horse like this one.

I ignite all 426 of my war horses under the purple hood, blowing fire out the intakes. I stamped the hell away from there like a scalded rabbit. Devastating sadness is riding like a tumor on my head, until I jam the gas. Plum Crazy jumps, and I start to feel better.

Hitting the cattle guard at 90 miles per hour, my tires smoking, and out onto the small paved highway, I am loving the instant fresh air and freedom from that place back there, you know the one. The tan brick one encasing the waxy families.

I haven't gone a 100 yards down that little blacktop country road, accelerating past 100 miles per hour, feeling so good to be away from that waxy death and all that it meant and portended, when I see a black state patrol car coming up behind me like a bat out of hell. He flips on his flashing red lights. I think, "Where the hell did I put Bob Wills Jr. telephone number?"

The stater went past me like I am frozen in time, in one of those glass cases at the heritage center back there. He looks over at me as he flies by. He uses his hands in that universal sign language, by pumping them up and down, palm down, "SLOW DOWN," he mouths, looking at me in the nano second I have available to see his face.

I hit my brakes as he disappears in the distance.

At 55 miles per hour I feel, what the… I could run this fast.

At 55 miles per hour, I have more time to think, though. I remember a beautiful quote from a Navajo friend, "On the beautiful trail I am, with it I wander."

I think about what I now know was called the Indian Heritage Center. Thinking back to that desolate place, I am somehow crushed by those wax people. If it had been a battle, waxy as they were, static as they were, they are inside my head, they would win.

The disparity between their glassy, sightless eyes and their gorgeous, original, actual historic handmade belongings was too much of a leap for me.

I try not to think of them, that sad, waxy family, askew, skewered on hidden spinal rods, alone at night.

With only a dim 40 watt distant electric lightbulb in a pale green hallway from a non-arcing, motionless summer moon, they are motionless for their eternity.

No evening soft gentle breezes there in that tan bricked government building. There will be no delighting there, no snorting pinto horses, no place to ride, anyway, even if they could, except up and down the waxed linoleum hallways. That sad little family is bricked in. There is nowhere to go. No children running through the village, shooting hoops, no laughing nursing mothers, no strong male voices. Who in that waxy group chips obsidian for arrow and spear points?

For sure there is not the sweet, smokey fragrance of a buffalo chip fire, a kettle of stewing buffalo meat with wild onions, and fragrant fry bread.

My warriors are active, running, jumping, moving, virile horsemen, shooters of rifles and bows. They are killers of running buffalo, up close and very personal. They also lure, by waving blankets, buffalo, by the thousands, off cliffs.

They are nomads, fearless, proud, feathered like the finest birds. They eat the still beating bloody buffalo heart.

Road trips come to you, you take whatever comes to you, or whatever you have the courage to engage with, or in. You have to participate, lead the way or stay home.

Gently rolling along at 55 mph, while Cuda takes a rest at slow speed, I look for a place to lunch. I see an opening off to my right in a barbed wire fence. I stop, back up. There is a rounded knoll with huge slabs of stone up on top, surrounded by a large golden cut wheat field. Pulling off, I drive up at an exaggerated angle, through wheat stubble up to a large pile of gigantic stones. They look like pages in a book laid down flat by ancient Gods.

I take a canvas bag from the car that Bob Wills Jr. gave to me. When he handed it to me, he winked as I was climbing into my car at the Bobcat, saying, "Here, eat more."

I manage to hoist Max high as the height of my shoulders, up on top of the biggest slab. I put the bag up beside Max, hearing the satisfying clink of a bottle.

Finding my way to the top of this great slab, I find Max is at the far end of the rock, staring out over an enthralling distant view. There are mountains, sharply etched, peaked and distant with a crenelated valley. Glistening, glittering in the very bottom, a winding river, bordered by quaking lustrous aspen, hazy, smokey, far off.

The top of the rock is covered with shells, snails, and trilobites embedded into the matrix of the solid stone. There is also a small circle of sheep skulls, with the remains of a fire in the center. Bird bones are scattered here and there. A few dried, dead sage bushes that tried to grow there once had died.

Sitting down on my old Hudson Bay four point looking out over this vast valley, it appears to have been ripped apart by some colossal hand filled with tectonic rage. Here, there, the distant peaks disappear, reappear in the blue-grey summer sunlit toasted fire smoke.

Somewhere out along the other side of the valley, a helicopter, its great bag of water on a long line. It slips, slides up distant smoking hills. I see, even at this great distance, the smoky pumpkin-colored hot sun flashing off its rotating blades, then it vanishes in the smoke, silently.

Patting my blanket, Max joins me, lying down, pressing against my thigh.

Grabbing my canvas bag, with large "Bobcat" printed on it, I look in. Oh my, that Bob Jr.

I find a pint of Evan Williams, 23 year old Kentucky bourbon whiskey. A medicine bottle filled with mineral waters for the whiskey.

Then, first wrapped in parchment, then foil, a generous slab of sumac seasoned elk steak, bone in. Sesame steamed carrots dusted with wasabi, cold steamed potatoes, all from last night's dinner. A generous hunk of homemade bread, a fruit jar of spring water and two glasses. One, a small Ridell tulip glass for the whiskey and the other a cut glass water goblet.

At the bottom, wrapped in a cotton towel, a small plastic box with a slice of boysenberry pie.

Under the towel, a small wooded cigar box, which, when I open it, I discover a box of wooden matches marked "Crillon Hotel,

Paris," a Cohiba cigar, and, wrapped in foil, a hand-rolled joint.

I lay back on the blanket, groaning. Holding my head, I sob. I just let it out. Tears run down my cheeks, into my ears, and into my mouth. I choke, coughing on the pain. Max licks my tears.

What is this litany of loneliness that pervades me? Did I go to it, or did it come to me? Who are we that in solitary inwardness that must be released or we rupture? Can anyone hear, me or is it only me weeping internally? Do I speak a language that anyone else can understand? Am I my own tower of Babel?

As the sun begins to set, the silver river turns to a river of gold.

Chanting liquid choruses, purling, bubbling, age old rivers flow in these tortured hills and mountains. For whatever reason, the sweet flowing sounds of brooks, creeks and rivers strike a memory cord in all mankind. I am struck.

"Once in his life a man ought to concentrate his mind upon the remembered earth, I believe. He ought to give himself up to a particular landscape in his experience, to look at it from as many angles as he can, to wonder about it, to dwell on it."

"How is it," I think, watching the evening sun begin to fall behind the far peak, "that people ride, drive, walk on this voluptuous Mother Earth, our Gaia, our earth goddess, in human form, yet know nothing about her? She can be read like a book."

"That is different from most women I have known," I think, laughing inwardly. Our solid Mother Earth bares great similarities to the foaming salt seas that rise and fall each day through the sensual gravitational pull of our other mother, Luna. She, with her two white horses and yoked chariot, drives across our skies each night.

This colossal stone slab I sit on with

Max is a petrified sea bottom, the prairie in front of me rolls like the sea. Locked into this solid rock are nektonic oracles from this distant pelagic sea that once filled the great bowl between the eastern Rocky Mountain front and the western Appalachian Mountains.

Sitting, watching Max intently gnawing a bone from the remains of the Elk steak, I look at my own hand.

What do most people, for that matter, know about their own bodies, their bones and pumping hearts, their muscles, the miles of arteries, the highways and byways of nerves? They only react. Ask anyone, "Where is your clavicle, or your patella, or your fibula?" Most, sadly, wouldn't have a clue.

Defense is a difficult game. Get behind the curve in a divorce, a game of chance, a business deal, or the game of life, you are still behind. Or, like Sisyphus, you can end up pushing a ceaseless death sentence, a boulder up a steep incline, perpetually.

Our unbridled loves, hates, pains, and joys, questions, and answers are cargo, which sneak out from pockets of self-deceit, and fulfilling passion.

Hidden in us, lethal and joyous, we are often defenseless to mental and physical ambushes.

It gets worse. How to anticipate jealousy, greed, envy, love, hate, how do we pre-empt it or embrace it?

"All I know is love, and I find my heart infinite and everywhere." In these mountains and rivers, this old ancient sea bed, I am in love.

What about her? "Perhaps the right moment comes when you have understood, without knowing why."

Hungry, I eat. I eat, so does Max. Thirsty, I drink. I drink, so does Max. Smokes, I smoke. Rolling into the warmth of my Hudsons Bay, curling Max into my arms, jacket for a pillow, I sleep. So does Max.

In the late morning, a small fire in the skull circle, elk on a stick, a carrot, a hot potato from the hot coals, fresh spring water, a small sip of whiskey, a hit for the road, then, off the rock and into Plumb Crazy.

Back on the road, in earthy bottom lands of dark opulent fertile earth, I see a wild rose, vermillion, fragrant, shy, and delicate. Stopping to smell its wild perfume, once again I am renewed. The road beckons.

I decide to drive at night for once, to avoid staters and log trucks. Also to stop often to look up into the heavens, without the ambient light of cities and towns. I vividly remember my dear, lovely mother standing in awe, looking into the night skies, saying, "Let nature be your teacher."

Flying softly through gently pine smoked airs, not another car on the road, I arrive at the outskirts of a small rural village.

At four in the morning, slowing to 10 miles per hour, foot off the gas pedal, coasting quietly, Cuda's deep throat grumbling at this reduced speed.

Driving down the dark main street when suddenly a nun, in white robes with a black hooded habit, steps purposefully right into the dark street and beckons, insisting that I stop.

At 10 miles per hour, in a town that is fast asleep, where even the barking dogs have stopped barking, a nun in a black with white hood stepping into your path is startling.

Behind her is a tall, sweet light with a yellow vaporous lamp, which gives her an orange halo.

A Madonna, beckoning with a pale white hand.

Her shape is vaguely bat shaped, her habit is pulled close, obscuring her ghostly pale face.

Her habit has black wings that make her darkened face look deep and mysterious. Something about her makes me think of the hooded grim reaper. The way her robes cling to her, it seems as if they are perhaps wet, a creepy feeling on a dry night.

Stopping, I roll down the passenger side window. She walks around from the front of the grunting Cuda, where I was forced to stop or run her over.

Leaning in with her forearms on the open window frame, I see she was smoking a hand rolled cigarette. I can't see her face except for her shinning dark eyes. I can't tell if she has been crying, or if they are only watering from the cool, early morning air.

"I need you to drive me somewhere," she says.

"Where is it you need to go?" I ask.

"Anywhere, just away from where I am standing," she says.

"Whats wrong with where you are?" I ask.

"Well," I say to her, "I don't know where I am going, I'm just going somewhere out there," pointing down the dark road ahead. Then I say. "You don't know me, why aren't you in church instead of being out on this road in the middle of the night? Are you running away from something, maybe the convent?"

"Do you always ask this many questions?" she asks.

No rejoinder, I just reach over, push open the passenger side car door, a beer can rolling out into the street. She climbs in.

"What the hell," she says, while trying to fit her feet in and around the garbage-strewn floor.

I look over at her and ask, "Whats the matter?"

"I have never seen so much shit in a

car, my feet don't even touch the floor. How long have you been running? What are you running from? I can feel your panic. You are running ahead of your demons."

Let's put it this way, I know I said I want questions, but just not that question.

A feeling of uselessness pervades my soul in front of this nun, this reservation white dove in nun's clothing, this apparition that is now flying around my car. She brings Jesus, what can I contribute but my grief? I will admit to a bit of self-pity. Well, really, if it is self-pity, deranged thinking, or the road, don't expect an answer.

I not so gently jam the gas pedal to the floor as we cross the cattle guard on the edge of town at 90 miles per hour. She is quiet, the cedar spicy scent of her perfume swirls in the car. One other thing swirls, her question.

I feel this pervading need to bury myself in the scents of this woman, as well as the smells of skunks, hay, feed lots, river bottoms, lighting strikes, and distant thunder.

Healing happens at our core.

Yet, as we pass 115 miles per hour, healing isn't happening. As we pass 118 miles per hour, I can feel the Cuda throatily opening all twin four barrel carbs. She stretches her legs, she loves to stretch herself. That purple girl of mine can run.

We enter into hyper reality where you know a little dip, a rise in the road. Was that a badger I just flashed by, minding its own business?

Then, there, hidden in a draw in the road, hidden in a dip in the single paved track, quietly walking, thinking of lush grassy meadows, and playful available cows, stands a large bull elk.

Illuminated in Cuda's headlights, there in the middle of the dark road, this elk appears with its great rack of horns flashing in the headlights.

No remote chance of stopping, this can, and most certainly will, leave me enmeshed in jagged plum crazy purple pieces of hot torn metal.

My severed ligaments, bones, and bone chips, my staring crushed skull, my horror stricken mouth ripped from ear to ear on the elk's rack, bleeding, my tongue a memory, lung sacs ripped open, nothing will survive.

Bits and pieces of my flesh, the nun's, and the elk's scattered hundreds of yards along the deserted road. On the road, off the road, end over end, showers of sparks, screeching, shrieking metal is being dragged along the old cracked paved roadway. No one, not out here, not 75 miles from services, hears anything, except perhaps a coyote half a mile away will hear the crash. Hearing this strange sound, he points his muzzle to the prairie sky, yowling.

When a tree falls in the forest, does it

make a sound?

Coming to a stop against a tectonic gigantic bit of ancient stone sea bed, all is quiet.

Then blood, freed from arteries, drips out of the mashed Cuda into the sagebrush and dusty earth.

Mixed in with the nun's blood, mine, the elk's, the engine oil, the high grade gasoline, all run, drip, coalesce with guts and bones, engine parts liberally mashed in, drip into the sage.

In a blinding flash, the whole smashed purple mess explodes sky ward.

The last of the elk steak, my two hundred year old buffalo skull (will the buffalo die again?), sweet sage bundles, dried frappuccino cups, feathers, books, the Tyto Alba Guttata lithograph, hawk feathers, receipts, all will go up in a radiant explosive pyre, as Cuda, tumbling like a reentry vehicle from space, spirals, a sickening dance, jumping, hopping, flame spreading across the high sage desert. Small fires ignite in the dry grass.

In the morning, all is quiet on the high desert's utterly deserted road. Under the charred, still smoldering, smoking remains, one can see an antique melted apple-green stem glass, fused with melted reading glasses for distance.

As I hit 123 miles per hour, I lose all mental control, my 1,000 pound foot, jammed on the gas pedal, also jams on my useless brain as thoughtless as approaching death.

Forgiveness (Can I forgive her? Can I forgive me?) flashes across my fervid glowing brain like forked lighting.

"Our memories are too frail a thread to hang our history from."

At this precise moment the nun slides over beside me, gently whispering, "It's all right, I'm not feeling that good myself. Why don't we think about this." She kisses my ear, my cheek, my flushed neck. "Lets pull over and let me hold you, what do you say?"

As we hurtle past 125 miles per hour, Cuda's loving it. She roars, bellows, happily howling, like a young lover's first wanton experience.

For that matter, what do cars know, inanimate objects that they are, about impending doom, with a distraught frenzied madman behind the wheel, calling down destruction?

Is this different than love or hate?

I am shouting, crying, and in my throat there is that ball, and when I try to swallow, it is still spitefully there.

The corners of my mouth pull down, my neck aches, by back kills me. I shout, "She's a bitch!"

Somewhere in the insanity I realize that if this darkened road turns, it's going to be rocks and gravel and dying, all in a flaming, doom-filled nano instant.

The nun softly, caressingly, slips her arm around me, kissing my neck, then my quivering throat, then puts her warm, moist tongue in my ear. I feel her hot breath.

These acts of kissing contract my foot from the gas pedal. Cuda slows, grumbling, then slows more. More grumbling from the torch hot 426, which is now shuttering the incoming air flow to the twin four barrel carburetors, until, putting my foot on the brake, Cuda slows, then stops on a small rise.

Reaching over, the nun shuts down the great V-8 engine. She then takes my head in her strong hands. I smell village camp fires. She turns my face toward hers, and kisses me deeply on my tear salted lips. I open my mouth, and she touches my tongue with hers. I bawl, sobbing.

She then turns, and with her lips points at the rising sun just below the chromed horizon, which is sending metallic orange Jesus rays skyward, dissipating the deep purple of the night sky. Stars start to disappear.

Sitting there, we watch the golden rim of the sun break the plane of the prairie with its luminous radiance.

The very essence of what we seek is our life energy, that essence is love. Love truly is light. From the goodness of love and light comes the essence of growth and goodwill.

As we watch the sun rise, its warmth brings understanding, and the acrid fear of darkness recedes. The nun, I see in the sunlight, is no longer a nun, rather a beautiful young Indian woman in a white elegant ski parka with a black mink fur trimmed hood.

"Let's walk," she said.

Getting out of Plum Crazy, which is still heated and popping, I put my arm around her strong, slender, supple waist while we walk toward the ascending morning sun.

Stopping now and then to kiss, murmuring words of understanding. Smitten by this beautiful young Indian woman, her hair, long, black like a raven's wing, I am lost and discovered, dreaming of sweet cypress scents, where my memory and the present collide, still tears in my eyes.

Healing is happening in this place where faces, hopes, and dreams come. Healing and restoration bring with it the twisting winds of warm, nourishing perfume, smells of summer wheat, redolent of these golden ripe dry lands.

A place of laughing children and loving women. Maybe I know where I am going.

There is that process of healing where passion gone dramatically awry resolves. The tormented turbulence abates.

As the screams of wind-driven grief calms, the rumbling of the tempestuous maelstrom grows faint. Small gusts swirl, eddy, then cats paws on small cat tail ponds gently ruffle, then calm, finally desire.

Our healing moments will be different for everyone, but perhaps this: a desire to arrange flowers. To feel sun on our uplifted faces. To freely laugh out loud, and feel it for its nurturing happiness. There is no longer the need to barricade ourselves from the respirating, oxygen depriving gray glare of nightmarish phantasms.

Believe, look around, "The old world's

the old world yet." You still have yourself, and what memories you want to keep, you own them, they are yours forever. What once was, will it never be again?

We are two little people walking in a vast sage desert towards the sunrise. We are both happy and afraid. We stop, tightly holding each, looking deeply into each others eyes, knowing that this moment is all that there is. That back there in my plum crazy Cuda is our other life. Back in the car, she will go her way, and I will go mine. I don't know her name, and never will. She will never know mine.

Miles Davis, great jazz trumpeter, once said, "What do we play? we play life."

Life is like this. Hold me a moment, a complete stranger sometimes, help me across to safety. Good Samaritans exist, simple as asking for help sometimes.

At times when we need someone to

help us across a river, we cling too tightly, and both drown.

That wasn't the case this time. I hold down a rusty barbed wire fence. Stepping over, we walk together, arms around each other's waist, to a little rise covered in small white fragrant flowers.

Stopping in that little garden of fragrance, she looks up at me as I hold her, asking, "Where are you going?"

I say, "I don't know. You?"

She says, "Off the reservation."

I lay out my large old wool Hudson Bay four point blanket, she folds her white parka for our pillow. Standing in the soul-stirring warm morning sun, we undress.

Somewhere, someone undresses so what?

THE END
'cuda

To author and artist Douglas Granum, creation is a way of life.

His inspiration is derived from his travels around the world and an appreciation of the unusual — trekking the jungles of New Guinea, enjoying plein aire painting in northern Urals of Russia, drifting down China's Yangtze River, looking at the stars in a Serengeti night sky, and commercial fishing in the storm-tossed Gulf of Alaska.

As an artist Douglas Granum works with and in various mediums including stone, metal, glass, wood, canvas, bronze and of course, writing. From creation in his studio in Southworth, Washington, his paintings, glass pieces, metal and stone sculptures can be found worldwide.

Find out more at DouglasGranum.com

Other stories by Douglas Granum:

JUDITH'S GAP

THE GERMAN MUSIC TEACHER'S COTTAGE

WAR NO PEACE

DEATH AND AFTERLIFE ON EL PASEO

OFF A LIGHT

THE ROSE COVERED COTTAGE

Find out more at DouglasGranum.com